S0-BEA-048

DISCARDED

Nashville Public Library | FOUNDATION

*This book given
to the Nashville Public Library
through the generosity of the*
**Dollar General
Literacy Foundation**

NPLF.ORG

MAXIMILIAN P. MOUSE, TIME TRAVELER

HEAD WEST, YOUNG MOUSE

TRANSCONTINENTAL RAILROAD TRAVELER

magic
wagon

BOOK 3

Philip M. Horender • Guy Wolek

visit us at www.abdopublishing.com

For my sisters, Heather & Wendy, who watched out for me growing up and whose friendship means so much now —PMH

Published by Magic Wagon, a division of the ABDO Group, PO Box 398166, Minneapolis, Minnesota 55439. Copyright © 2014 by Abdo Consulting Group, Inc. International copyrights reserved in all countries. All rights reserved. No part of this book may be reproduced in any form without written permission from the publisher.

Calico Chapter Books™ is a trademark and logo of Magic Wagon.

Printed in the United States of America, North Mankato, Minnesota.
052013
092013
 This book contains at least 10% recycled materials.

Text by Philip M. Horender
Illustrations by Guy Wolek
Edited by Stephanie Hedlund and Rochelle Baltzer
Cover and interior design by Neil Klinepier

Library of Congress Cataloging-in-Publication Data
Horender, Philip M.
  Head west, young mouse : transcontinental railroad traveler / by Philip M. Horender ; illustrated by Guy Wolek.
    p. cm. -- (Maximilian P. Mouse, time traveler ; bk. 3)
  Summary: Maximilian finds himself in a wagon traveling west with a prairie dog named Madeline, and witnessing the driving of the "golden spike" and the completion of the transcontinental railroad in 1869--and incidentally preventing a pair of thieves from making off with a nice couple's wagon and supplies.
  ISBN 978-1-61641-959-2
1. Mice--Juvenile fiction. 2. Prairie dogs--Juvenile fiction. 3. Time travel--Juvenile fiction. 4. Railroads--United States--History--19th century--Juvenile fiction. 5. Frontier and pioneer life--Juvenile fiction. 6. Utah--History--Juvenile fiction. [1. Mice--Fiction. 2. Prairie dogs--Fiction. 3. Animals--Fiction. 4. Time travel--Fiction. 5. Adventure and adventurers--Fiction. 6. Railroads--United States--History--19th century--Fiction. 7. Frontier and pioneer life--Fiction. 8. Utah--History--Fiction.] I. Wolek, Guy, ill. II. Title.
  PZ7.H78087He 2013
  813.6--dc23
                                    2012050547

TABLE OF CONTENTS

Chapter 1:
AROUND THE FIRE

Maximilian opened his sleepy eyes. They were swollen and sore from crying. His stomach growled. It suddenly dawned on him that he wasn't moving and it was **eerily** quiet. He carefully got to his paws and went toward the slit in the tarp.

It was dark outside when Maximilian pulled the heavy cloth drape open and peered out. He gazed at a star-filled sky unlike anything he had ever seen before. Several campfires burned nearby.

It must have been late evening because only a small group of people were awake. They talked quietly around the fires.

Maximilian was on a mission to save his home in Tanner's Glen. When he learned that Farmer Tanner was being foreclosed on, he

4

knew he had to do something as mouse of the house. He had met Nathaniel Chipmunk III and borrowed Nathaniel's time machine.

The time machine had taken Maximilian back in time to Boston in 1773 and then to Gettysburg in 1863. Maximilian had tried a third time to get home. Now, he shivered as the night breeze chilled his bones. If the newspaper he had discovered was recent, it was 1869.

Before thinking twice, Maximilian scurried down the rear hatch of the wagon. He ran

around the rim of the wooden-spoked wheel to the hard ground below.

Maximilian moved closer to one of the fires. He listened to two men. One of the men was carving a piece of wood. The other was carefully reading a map that had been unrolled on a large slab of bedrock.

Maximilian inched closer. The low rustling of horse hooves could be heard behind him. He wanted to get a look at the map.

"If this map is **accurate**, then we're still two days east of Silver Springs," the man said.

The other man kept carving, but nodded in agreement. "That's about right," he said. "So long as the axle on the Franklin wagon is fixed, we should be in decent shape."

The man reading the map moved to stir a kettle that hung over the fire. He placed his tattered cowboy hat on the ground.

"I just hope that the Utah Territory is more agreeable than Missouri was," he said.

Both men sat quietly beneath the vast prairie sky and thought about what was in store for them. Maximilian did the same.

Chapter 2:
CHECKING THINGS OUT

Maximilian P. Mouse had a favorite time of day. It was dawn, just before the sun rose.

It was this time that the wagon train stretched as far as the eye could see across the Midwestern plains. Maximilian sat at the rear of the covered wagon. He watched the **caravan** snake its way over the vast countryside. He couldn't help but be amazed at what an impressive sight it truly was.

The large, soft brown ox that followed his wagon chewed her cud. Then, she gave Maximilian an uneasy stare.

Maximilian knew it was rare that larger, stronger animals were frightened by smaller field mice. But, he had certainly met his fair share that were scared by him.

Maximilian felt somewhat guilty that he was riding in the wagon in front of the ox. So, he gave her a friendly wave and smiled at her. She smiled back and blew away a pesky fly.

The paths the wagons traveled over were hardly roads. They were really just trails. This particular one looked as if it hadn't been used in months. The wagons jostled and rocked violently.

Maximilian was careful not to get too close to the edge of the wagon's gate. He clung tightly to a leather strap attached to the overhanging tarp. He checked on the time machine once in a while. It seemed to be working, but that did little to calm Maximilian's nerves. He feared it would tip over completely.

Without warning, the wagon came to a stop. The wagons behind them did as well. The man driving the wagon behind them hopped from his wooden bench. He patted his cowboy hat against his leg.

"We're making good time," he announced, looking to the sky for the position of the sun.

A woman appeared from behind the wagon. She was wearing a light yellow bonnet and a soft blue dress. Long, caramel brown hair framed her face from underneath her bonnet. She carried a pail of water and a ladle. Her face was kind and youthful and she spoke softly as she walked to the head of the wagon.

"You must be awfully **parched**, Robert," she said, handing the man the ladle. She was careful not to let any water spill.

"Much **obliged**, Martha," Robert said, putting the spoon to his mouth. Sweat glistened on his brow as he drank from the ladle.

Maximilian could imagine how cold and refreshing the water was. He was reminded of how hot and thirsty he had become. He licked his lips.

"How is Caroline holding up?" Robert asked. He placed the sweat-stained hat back on his head.

"Caroline's fine, just fine," Martha responded. "She never complains."

"Well, it sure will feel good when we finally reach Silver Springs," Robert said. He gave Maximilian's ox friend a playful pat on the side. "Gabe talked to some **prospectors** two days ago. They said the panning was picking back up and railroad jobs were available."

"Well, as long as we're together everything will be fine," Martha said. Her voice sounded almost like she was singing. Maximilian liked them.

Robert gave Martha a loving kiss on the forehead. Then, he climbed back onto his seat in the wagon.

"You always know the right thing to say, my sweet Martha," Robert said, taking the oxen team's reins in his hands.

As Martha turned, Maximilian noticed something—or someone to be exact. A small, blonde animal sat at the base of the rear wheel. Sitting motionless underneath the wagon, no one saw her. No one, that is, except Maximilian.

Chapter 3:
A BUMPY RIDE

With a violent jolt, the caravan was again moving forward. Maximilian wondered how long it would be until the next break. He thought he had plenty of time to explore the wagon a little more. So, he made his way toward the front.

Maximilian wandered through a maze of boxes. He carefully read their written labels. Bedding . . . kitchen . . . tools . . . garden . . .

One box in particular caught the attention of his nose. Maximilian paused to peer inside it. He drew in a long, deep sniff of dried basil and salted beef.

He thought for a moment of helping himself. What would his mother say if she knew he was taking food from families he didn't know? He had already done enough on his trip that his mother certainly would not have agreed with.

Maximilian decided to keep moving. He could hear muffled voices coming from the wagon's drivers. He walked slowly so he wouldn't lose his balance.

Finally, Maximilian was able to brace himself on a nearby shovel. He listened closer to the two men. Immediately, it became clear that one of the men was suffering from some kind of sickness.

"We need a little bit of luck with those clouds to make it to camp by nightfall," the man managed to say between painful coughs.

"The valley we were told about shouldn't be too far away. Who knows what the weather will be on the other side," the driver replied. "We've been pretty fortunate so far."

The wagon swayed beneath Maximilian's paws. Suddenly, he heard a loud crash behind him. He looked back, fearful that it had been the time machine. But only a jar of pickled eggs was shattered over the stained, wooden floorboards.

Maximilian couldn't see the two men who were talking. But, their **silhouettes** stretched over the wagon's canvas from the late afternoon sun. The one who had taken ill often sipped from a **canteen** hidden in his breast pocket.

The driver snapped the reins of the horses and quickened their pace. "As concerned as I am with that storm front, I'm more worried about that cough," he said.

"Don't worry about me, Garvey," the man said. "If this fever would break, I think this cough would improve."

A breeze swept through the wagon and cooled Maximilian's warm cheeks. He closed his eyes and imagined himself standing in the grassy meadow outside Tanner's Glen. He remembered the cool summer winds hitting his face and playing with his whiskers.

"Whoa!" the wagon conductor said in a low voice. The rusted axles ground to a halt.

"Well, it looks like our luck finally ran out. We're not going to have to worry about making it to that valley," Garvey said in frustration.

His friend coughed and struggled to catch his breath. "That Franklin wagon is going to be the death of all of us. We should leave them out here to fend for themselves."

"Don't go talking crazy now, Hal. We'll manage to fix it again. If we have to camp before the valley, so be it," Garvey said, reaching behind him. He unexpectedly grabbed the shovel that was supporting Maximilian.

Maximilian imagined how frustrating this process must be for everyone. It did, however, provide him with the opportunity to investigate his mystery friend.

Maximilian hurried to the wagon's gate and made his way to the ground. It was so dirty on the trail that dust actually seemed to hang in the air like the seeds from a dandelion. Maximilian removed his pocket watch and brushed the dust from its face.

To Maximilian's amazement, it was almost two o'clock. He estimated that he had arrived shortly after midnight. He had only ten hours or so before he could test his luck yet again with the time machine.

Maximilian was sure this stop would not be as eventful as Boston and Gettysburg had been. He made his way to the next wagon in the caravan, determined to find out more about the animal who had caught his eye.

Chapter 4:
MADELINE

To Maximilian's surprise, the wagon behind his lay broken on the prairie. A splintered axle was ten yards behind them. Apparently, the Robert and Martha that Maximilian had seen during their last stop were the Franklins. They were the same people that Garvey and Hal had been talking about.

Maximilian walked carefully around the accident. He hid under the half of the wagon still standing on two steel-rimmed wheels.

"We're so close," Martha said, beginning to sob. "I thought you said it was fixed."

Robert leaned over to take a closer look at the wagon. "It could be worse, Martha," he said in a calm, composed tone. "The rest of the wagon seems to be holding up. If we could just build a makeshift axle that could tolerate

this path. We only have a few hundred more miles to go."

Maximilian watched as Garvey and Hal reached the Franklin wagon. He wondered why Garvey had the small wooden shovel slung over his shoulder.

"This cart of yours is really starting to hold up progress, Rob," Garvey said. He turned his head and spit on the ground. Maximilian cringed in disgust.

Meanwhile, Hal was watching the sky. He could see clouds approaching from the south. He was sweating, his skin pale. Maximilian knew he was sick, but he had no idea it was this bad.

"My patience has run out with you, Franklin," Hal said as raindrops started to pelt the ground around them. "We could lose our lives because of your busted axle."

Maximilian could hear the rain come down harder as the sky turned an angry black. He watched the men attempt to free the wagon and organize their belongings for camp. Maximilian was so focused, he failed to see the small prairie dog next to him. Her paws were full of bags.

"Excuse me," the short-haired prairie dog said. "If you haven't noticed, it's starting to rain."

A startled Maximilian jumped and stepped to the side. The prairie dog tossed a heavy knapsack on the ground in a cloud of dust. She carefully removed another bag from her back and placed that on the ground as well.

"What's the matter?" she asked, staring at Maximilian. "You've never see a prairie dog before?"

Maximilian paused for a moment and responded quite bluntly, "Actually, no."

The prairie dog managed a friendly smile that softened her eyes. "Listen, it's been a long day," she said. She positioned herself on the ground next to her bags. "It's been a long month, come to think of it."

Maximilian glanced at her bags. The few she had were bulging at the seams. Maximilian wondered how long she had been traveling and where she was coming from.

"My name's Maximilian," he said shyly, looking down at her. Her eyelashes were long and curled. Her nose was a pastel pink. His heart fluttered as she looked back at him.

"I'm Madeline," she said. She extended her paw in his direction.

Maximilian stood frozen. His throat was dry and his mind failed to make his mouth move.

"It's customary that when one animal extends his or her paw, you make his or her **acquaintance** by doing the same," the prairie dog teased.

"I'm sorry," Maximilian stammered. He shook her paw. His cheeks were warm. Even though it was getting darker every minute, he was sure she could see him blushing.

Chapter 5:
THE OLD SPANISH TRAIL

Soon, the wagon caravan was circled and the tents were set up. No one noticed the small fire burning underneath the crippled Franklin wagon. Maximilian and Madeline sat warming their paws by the flames.

"It was a good idea to get the fire started before the ground got too damp, Madeline," Maximilian said. He blew warm air into his hands.

"It's amazing how cold it can get here once the sun goes down. It's so hot during the day," Madeline said.

"Have you been traveling with the Franklins long?" Maximilian asked. He wanted to avoid any awkward silences.

"Hmm," she said. She shook her head and dug through one of her bags. Madeline removed a saltine cracker and offered half to Maximilian.

"Thank you so much," Maximilian said, taking a bite.

"I met the Franklins a couple of weeks ago outside of Norman, Oklahoma," Madeline replied.

"I'm originally from the Oklahoma Territory," she said. She sat staring into the orange flames that licked the night air. "The Franklins are from Missouri. They were passing through Norman on their way to Silver Springs."

Maximilian's head was spinning with all of the different places and names. He was curious to know if they were close to Boston or Gettysburg. But he didn't want to ask.

"Like a lot of other wagon trains, the Franklins met up with all of these other settlers at Elm Grove, Missouri. They elected their captains, guides, and other officers. Then, they began their long trek westward," Madeline said.

"They began their trip on the Oregon Trail," she continued. "Later, they picked up the Old Spanish Trail. The Old Spanish Trail hasn't been used as much. It is really rough and bumpy."

Maximilian could agree with that. His body was sore from all of the jarring during his short ride. He wondered whether it would get any better.

"I don't understand why they chose this trail," Madeline said. She was aware that Maximilian was listening closely to her every word. "The Old Spanish Trail was rarely traveled by wagons like these. Up until now, most of the travelers using this route have been Mexican pack trains."

A strong breeze blew through the spokes of one of the wagon's wheels. It threatened to put out their small fire. Maximilian moved to try to protect the source of their light and heat.

"It is hard to say how many wagons have made this trip. More and more people came each year between 1843 and 1848," Madeline said. She drew her coat tighter around her. Her tail was shorter than Maximilian's, but it was much fuller and furrier. Maximilian was envious of how warm it seemed to be.

"How do you know all of this, Madeline?" Maximilian asked. "I feel like I'm listening to my schoolteacher."

Madeline gave Maximilian an almost embarrassed look. She opened one of the heavy bags she had been toting. It was full of books.

"I love to read," she said meekly. "I always have, ever since I was little."

Maximilian's eyes got big when he saw the number of books she had been traveling with. Many were hard-covered and leather bound.

"That sack must be extremely heavy!" Maximilian said.

"It is, but I simply cannot bring myself to part with any of them," Madeline replied. "I've read all of them. Many of them I've read more than once."

"I enjoy reading, too," Maximilian said. "I've been keeping a journal of my journey. I include all of the people I meet and all of the places I visit."

"I'm impressed!" Madeline said. "A lot of the books I've read about **pioneers** headed West have been journals. I love reading about someone who's actually experienced these adventures firsthand."

The rain seemed to be letting up. But, the dampness continued to surround their campsite.

"I feel such a connection to the people I read about, that I never feel alone," Madeline said. "The characters in my books really helped me get through some difficult times. Does that sound foolish, Maximilian?" she asked.

"No," Maximilian said. "No, it doesn't. It's nice to know that you're never alone."

The fire seemed to finally be warming the small mouse and his new friend. The two sat enjoying each other's company and the crackling campfire. Maximilian added a few more blades of the tough prairie grass. Despite the weather, he felt warm and safe.

Maximilian glanced at his pocket watch. He saw that it was early morning. The time machine would be ready to try again shortly.

"Maybe someday you'll write about me in your journal, Maximilian," Madeline said softly, breaking the silence.

"I think someday I probably will," he answered. He passed her part of his cracker.

Chapter 6:
A MISSING WAGON

The morning sun announced its arrival with beautiful red and orange clouds. Maximilian opened his eyes. Madeline was curled in a tight ball next to the dying fire.

Madeline had fallen asleep first last night, Maximilian recalled. Using one of her bags as a pillow, he had fallen asleep soon after.

The morning brought with it some much needed warmth. Maximilian stretched and yawned. It was quiet in the camp, except for a rustling of feet at the front of the caravan.

Suddenly, panicked shouts cut through the silence of the early dawn. Maximilian and Madeline were both startled. They jumped to their feet.

"They're gone!" Robert Franklin yelled.

Maximilian craned his neck and turned his ears. He tried to find out what was happening. But he could only see feet running from his spot underneath the wagon.

"Robert, calm down," a man said, breathing hard. "Who's gone?"

"Garvey and Hal must have left last night," Robert finally managed to say. Maximilian and Madeline stared at one another in shock. "And they took the wagons and teams with them!"

Maximilian lost himself for a moment and ran into the open. Madeline called to him as he stepped out into the bright sunlight.

The man who Maximilian had seen looking at the map had thrown his hat on the ground. Now he was staring at it in disbelief.

"Are you sure, Robert?" he asked. "How far could they have gotten?"

Robert was angry. He kicked his damaged wagon. Luckily, Madeline had moved under a different wagon and now watched from a safe distance.

Martha had appeared holding the hand of a small girl. Her strawberry-blonde hair played wistfully in the breeze.

Maximilian ran, although he didn't know exactly where he was going. He just had to find the wagon that contained the time machine.

"Martha," Robert said, "they stole our second wagon and the horses." He wasn't yelling anymore. He had stopped pacing. The child, who cradled a tattered doll tight to her chest, began to cry.

Maximilian's eyes darted from one wagon to another. They all looked the same to him. But he was certain the covered wagon he had arrived in last night was gone.

"The wagons and the horses are gone," Robert repeated.

"The time machine is gone," Maximilian said. He dropped to his knees.

Chapter 7:
OPEN PRAIRIE

Maximilian opened his eyes. They were sore from how hard he had pressed them together. He walked back to the Franklin wagon and gathered his things.

Garvey and Hal had stolen two wagons full of supplies and items belonging to the Franklin family. They also took four horses. This got the other pioneers moving. They all worked **frantically** to gather their belongings and pack their wagons.

"What are you going to do, Maximilian?" Madeline asked.

"I don't know," Maximilian responded with frustration. "My only way home was on that wagon," he said. He didn't know whether to cry or scream.

"There are other wagons, Maximilian," Madeline said, trying to comfort her friend.

"You don't understand," Maximilian said. Maximilian tied his overcoat around his waist and rolled up his sleeves. He stepped onto the open prairie. He looked around and tried to determine which direction the thieves might have headed.

"What do you think you're doing?" Madeline asked with a chuckle.

"I'm going to find Garvey and Hal," Maximilian said. He began walking in the direction he thought was west. Based on the position of the sun, he had a good idea of which way they had been traveling since yesterday.

"Don't be silly!" Madeline exclaimed. "You would only last a few hours in the wide-open prairie on your own! Have you seen the hungry vultures circling above our wagons every time we stop to camp?"

Maximilian stopped.

"Besides, Robert Franklin has managed to fashion himself another axle. Once they get that wheel fixed, they'll be after those two bandits themselves," Madeline said.

Maximilian knew that she was right. He wouldn't last through the day on his own. He knew that he had a better chance of finding Garvey and Hal and the time machine if he stuck with the rest of the caravan.

"It will be alright, Maximilian," Madeline continued as he walked slowly back to her.

In that short period of time, Robert and some other men had managed to jack up the wagon several inches. They were making the proper repairs.

Maximilian thought about what Madeline had said. Robert and the others would never allow Garvey and Hal to get away with this.

Chapter 8:
RIDING ALONG

Within the hour, the caravan was back on track. The group was moving west toward the blazing hot sun. Not a cloud was in sight. Maximilian looked toward the heavens to offer up a wish, or a prayer, for help finding the stolen time machine.

Maximilian rode quietly with Madeline in the rear of the Franklins' wagon. The broken axle had been repaired yet again. But all of the gear had been emptied into other wagons to lessen its load.

Madeline opened one of her books. She cleared her throat in an attempt to get Maximilian's attention. She wanted to take his mind off of his worries.

"Would you like to hear more about the pioneers who have gone before us on these trails?" she asked.

Maximilian tried not to smile, but he couldn't help it. The truth was, listening to her stories of others overcoming hardships gave him hope.

"That would be fine," Maximilian said.

Madeline was excited by his response. She touched her finger to her tongue and turned to a page with a creased corner.

"Oh, here we are," Madeline said. "You will surely enjoy hearing this one."

Maximilian listened closely as she read.

"During the 1850s, caravans large and small were paving paths throughout the Great Plains," Madeline began. "A man by the name of Randolph B. Marcy conducted a **convoy** of 100 wagons from Fort Smith, Arkansas, to the New Mexico Territory via the Canadian River in 1849."

Madeline paused for a moment, her gaze falling on Maximilian.

"A hundred wagons strong!" she said in astonishment. "Can you imagine?"

"How many wagons do we have in this caravan?" Maximilian asked. He looked out past the rear tarp at the line of wagons and carts behind them.

"I last counted thirty-six total," Madeline said. "Of course, that was back in Oklahoma. And, it was before Garvey and Hal decided to break away from the others."

Maximilian nodded and sighed.

"You know, Maximilian," Madeline said in a stern voice, "every person that you see in this caravan has had to overcome hurdles. They have had to keep faith that things would work out."

Maximilian heard what Madeline was saying. He had to admit he was **wallowing** a little.

"The Franklins' little girl, the one you saw crying," Madeline continued, "she had friends she left behind in Missouri. She had just started to attend a school, too. This is the very first time I've seen a tear on that sweet child's cheek."

"What about you, Madeline?" Maximilian asked cautiously. She had told him a lot about the history of the West and the brave settlers who had risked everything in their journeys across it. But he still knew very little about her story. "If you were to compose a book telling your story, what might it say?"

Madeline looked away from Maximilian. She turned to the pages of her history book.

"I wonder how far ahead Garvey and Hal have managed to get," Madeline said, avoiding the question.

"I'm sorry," Maximilian said, feeling embarrassed. "I was out of place in asking."

"No, that's okay, Maximilian," Madeline said, shaking her head. "Here I am lecturing you on the hardships others have overcome and I can't even talk about my own past."

Maximilian took another one of her books in his lap and carefully peeled back the cover.

"How about this book?" he said innocently. "What was this book about?"

Madeline wiped a tear from her fur, her face flushed red. "This one?" she said. "This book is one of my favorites!"

Chapter 9:
SILVER SPRINGS

The band of wagons slowly made their way into the boomtown of Silver Springs, Utah. At dusk, they arrived in the center of the settlement.

Amazingly, time had gone fast in Madeline's company. Maximilian's pocket watch chimed seven in the evening.

"You better keep that watch of yours close, Maximilian," Madeline warned. She tied her own bags tightly and pulled them close.

"Why's that?" Maximilian asked.

Madeline peered out the back of the wagon suspiciously. They were attracting the attention of several men sitting on the stoops of some local businesses.

"These towns are **notorious** for drifters," Madeline whispered to Maximilian. "The silver and gold booms have reached these places. The railroads are beginning to find their way here, too. But the law is nowhere to be seen."

Maximilian made sure the chain linking his precious watch to his coat pocket was secure.

"In fact, I wouldn't at all be surprised to find Garvey and Hal have slithered their way into a town like this," she said. "Those snakes."

This got Maximilian's attention.

Silver Springs certainly was not the bustling center that Boston was. It wasn't even the pleasant town that Gettysburg had been. Outlined on the bleak landscape of the Utah plains, Silver Springs had only a handful of businesses.

The wagon limped past a bank, a general store named Floyd's **Mercantile**, a saloon named The Tumbleweed, and several other generic-looking buildings. At the end of the town's main strip was a two-story hotel.

The Franklin wagon slowly came to a halt. Robert jumped from his seat to hitch the team to a post out front of the hotel. Most of the other wagons continued past. They moved to an open field some twenty yards outside of town.

"Robert, what are we doing here?" Martha asked. "Aren't we going to join the others?"

Madeline was organizing her book bag while Maximilian was surveying the town. He watched some people pulling carts with mining equipment. Others rode in search of food as the sun set on another day in Silver Springs.

"I'll be joining the others once I get you settled in your room!" Robert exclaimed to his wife.

He took his wife's hand and led her to the front of the hotel. Removing his hat, he opened the door for Martha. Then, he motioned with his other hand for her to go inside.

Maximilian and Madeline were still in the rear of the wagon.

"Is this like other towns that the wagon train has stopped in?" Maximilian asked Madeline.

"To be quite honest, we haven't stopped for some time now," she said. She seemed somewhat distracted.

Maximilian followed her gaze into the distance just beyond Floyd's Mercantile.

"Do you hear that?" Madeline asked with a broad smile.

Maximilian strained to hear over the noise of passing cowboys and their horses.

"I can hear running water, I think," Maximilian said, unsure of himself.

Madeline got to her feet and tied the strings of her bag tightly.

"Have you ever panned for gold, Maximilian?" Madeline asked.

Maximilian shook his head. "I can't say I have," he said.

"Well, tomorrow you will," Madeline declared. She began to make her way to the ground.

Chapter 10

A NIGHT AT THE OASIS

The Oasis Hotel in Silver Springs, Utah, was not a fancy establishment. But, it certainly was better than sleeping outdoors or under the Franklin family wagon.

The hotel lobby was simple. It had a brass chandelier, complete with cobwebs and a layer of dust. There was also a counter with a bell, which was to be rung if the attendant was not present. A player piano sat in the corner.

Maximilian was somewhat amazed that a piano was in the lobby. It looked as though it hadn't been played in ages. It was currently serving as a bookshelf with a number of old books and newspapers sitting on the keys.

The hotel was not much to look at. But, Maximilian was sure that Robert Franklin had paid a lot of money for his wife to have a mattress and washroom of her own. It also meant that Maximilian and Madeline would have a place to stay.

The hotel manager was more interested in returning to his card game in the inn's office than registering guests. He was more than happy to take Robert's money but didn't help them with Martha's bags.

Martha's room was located on the second floor. Robert grabbed a tattered suitcase and a floral handbag and they made their way to the second landing. Maximilian and Madeline followed. They struggled to get their belongings up the flight of stairs.

The hallway their room was located in had several **kerosene** lamps. A pair of spurs hung on one wall, while a framed map of the Utah Territory hung on the other.

"Can you make out anything on that map?" Madeline asked quietly.

The map was yellowed and the light in the hallway wasn't very good. But Maximilian was able to make out a few locations.

"Someone has circled Silver Springs," Maximilian said, squinting in the darkness. "I can see that we're close to a place called Promontory Point. A little bit farther is a larger town named Salt Lake City."

Madeline shook her head. "I've heard some of the men in our caravan talk about Salt Lake City. I've read about it in a number of my books, too," she said.

She tugged at his coat sleeve.

"Come on, the door to our room is open," Madeline said. "Hurry! We don't want to be stuck in this hallway for the night."

The two of them scurried into room twenty-one. They hid under a bedside table that held a lantern and a book of matches. Robert Franklin carefully removed the lantern's glass and lit the wick.

"What do you think, Martha?" Robert asked. Maximilian could hear the pride in his voice.

"This is really too much, Robert," she said. "I would be more than content with you and Caroline out in the wagon."

"Nonsense," Robert said. "You've been so strong throughout this entire trip. You deserve to get a good night's sleep in a real bed."

"It's too much though," Martha continued. "This hotel is too expensive. We're going to need to be **frugal** until you find a job with the railroad."

"We're fine, Martha," Robert said. He placed his hands on her shoulders. "The man downstairs said that Union Pacific has a headquarters in town. Come sun up, I'll go and get a job."

"You've done such a good job getting our family to this point, Robert," Martha said. She sat on the queen-sized bed with her purse in her lap.

Robert placed his hat back on his head and moved toward the door.

"This is just the beginning," he said, looking at her adoringly. "It's a new beginning for us and for Caroline. I'll be right outside if you need anything."

Martha smiled and ran her hand over the bedspread.

"Make sure you lock this door when I leave," Robert said. Martha did as he said before retiring for the night.

Maximilian and Madeline sat awake for a few minutes after Martha had blown out the light.

"What's our plan, Maximilian?" Madeline whispered.

"I guess we start looking for Garvey and Hal and the stolen wagons," he responded. He sat with his back relaxed against the wall. The warmth of the room made him tired.

"They must be here somewhere," Madeline said. She wrapped her tail around her and closed her eyes.

The streets of Silver Springs were full of **commotion** and rowdy men looking to strike it rich. Maximilian felt safe in the hotel room. He slowly fell asleep. After all, there would be plenty of time to worry about finding the time machine tomorrow.

Chapter 11:
PANNING FOR GOLD

The following morning brought another hot, dry day to Silver Springs. A heavy cloud of dust made it difficult for Maximilian and Madeline to cross the street. At the same time, Robert Franklin made his way with several other men to the office of the Union Pacific Railroad Company.

"Do you know how Silver Springs got its name?" Madeline asked, refreshed. The hotel room had provided a solid night's sleep. They had awakened to the hustle and bustle of merchants opening their doors and cattlemen loading their feed.

"I assumed that the town's name came from the silver mines in the surrounding hillsides that Robert spoke of," Maximilian responded with certainty.

Maximilian and Madeline saw a slight opening in the street's traffic and sprinted full speed to the other side.

"Ha!" Madeline said, breathing heavily. "That's precisely what I thought as well," she said. "I read a chapter in one of my books this morning before you woke. It mentioned the streams and rivers that flow through the Utah landscape. The water is so clear in some spots that early settlers had remarked that it reminded them of silver."

Maximilian thought for a moment about the creeks that bordered the Tanner farmstead. They were muddy and murky, especially after the spring rains.

The mouse and prairie dog continued to walk. They enjoyed the early morning sunshine and each other's company. Soon, they were leaving the township behind them.

Small shrubs and bushes now dotted the countryside. The land was nothing like what

Maximilian was used to. But he found it very peaceful and beautiful.

Almost 100 yards from the Oasis Hotel, there was a stream with a sandy riverbank. It seemed quite out of place considering how bleak the nearby town was. Maximilian immediately noticed how brilliantly clear the water was. With his fur covered in a heavy layer of dust, he fought the urge to take an early morning swim.

Madeline reached inside her coat pocket and revealed two small copper coins. They were bent and curved on all sides. In fact, they were so bent that they barely looked like coins at all.

"Here," she said, handing Maximilian one of the pieces. "I've only done this once before and it's been awhile," Madeline continued. "We had made a weekend stop along the Butte River in Nebraska because one of the women we were traveling with was having a baby."

The coin felt surprisingly light in Maximilian's paw. It was so bowed it looked like a pan. From what Maximilian gathered, that's exactly what Madeline had wanted.

"Panning for gold is quite simple, Maximilian," Madeline said. She bent at the river's edge and dipped the front of her coin into the shallow pool. "Your coin will act as your pan. In it, you'll try to re-create what Mother Nature does herself in the riverbeds."

Maximilian shook his head. It sounded so easy. He watched as Madeline began to let the cool, crisp water make its way into the bottom of her coin.

Since he had started his journey in the time machine, Maximilian had been trying desperately to get to the correct time and location. But he had spent almost no time creating a plan to actually save Tanner's Glen when he got there.

A part of him felt guilty being out here with Madeline. What was he doing panning for gold? Then it occurred to him—this could actually be the key to saving his home! Gold was valuable. He could bring it back with him and save Tanner's Glen.

Maximilian bent down next to Madeline. He dipped the edge of his coin into the water, shadowing what she did.

"Alright, Madeline," Maximilian said, "how am I supposed to do this?"

Chapter 12:
STRATIFYING

"You want to make sure that you're in a good spot to do your panning," Madeline began. She watched the water and the flow of its current. "You should choose a location where the water is not too deep. It should also move rapidly enough to keep the water clear."

Maximilian surely did not want to pan in water that was too deep. Just the thought of losing his footing or getting caught in the current made him nervous. He was beginning to understand what Madeline was saying. They seemed to be in a good place already.

"We're fortunate to have such clean, clear water," Madeline said. "You don't want to wash away a big nugget of gold!"

"The next tool we need is a piece of screen. Panners refer to it as a **sieve**," Madeline said. She reached into her pocket for the second time. She revealed two small pieces of mesh. Each was small enough to fit just inside the lip of the coin's curved rims.

"I helped myself to some of the screen in Martha Franklin's hotel room this morning," Madeline said with a sheepish grin. "Don't tell anyone."

Maximilian removed his jacket and placed it on a nearby rock. He decided he would wash it in the river before they left. For now, he rolled up the sleeves of his shirt and waded ankle deep into the refreshingly chilly river water.

"How am I doing?" Maximilian asked Madeline. She was located a few yards from him upstream.

"You might just be a natural at this, Maximilian," she said, starting the panning process herself.

"Submerge your coin just below the brim and shake it side to side," Madeline said. She showed him how to do it as she described it to him. "Be very careful not to wash a lot of material out of your coin when you're doing this," she warned.

"Anything heavy in your water will work its way to the bottom of your pan. The lighter, less valuable material will rise to the top."

"This isn't too hard," Maximilian said quietly to himself. He concentrated on every direction Madeline gave. After a while, it became clear that patience was going to be needed that day.

Maximilian and Madeline worked quietly for a few minutes. The occasional birdcall overhead was the only break in the silence.

"I once read a guidebook written by a gold prospector. He came to this area of the country in the early 1840s. He called this process *stratifying*," Madeline finally said. "He wrote that you shouldn't be shy about getting your paws in the wet material to break it up. You have to be sure to rinse off any of the larger stones and to break up any clay balls or roots."

Beads of sweat began to form on Maximilian's forehead in the rising Utah sun. He was working hard stratifying like Madeline said. He was trying even harder to ignore the

feeling of disappointment that was beginning in the core of his stomach.

Maximilian had thought this would be a lot more rewarding.

"Am I doing something wrong?" Maximilian asked.

"No," Madeline called back. "I've been watching you and you're doing very well. Try not to get frustrated. Many people spend a lot of time doing what we are and never find anything."

Maximilian's heart sank. A lot was riding on him finding some gold, regardless of how small. He took a minute to wipe his brow with his handkerchief. Then, he went back to work stratifying.

Madeline let out an excited scream and Maximilian jumped.

"Come here!" she cried. "I think I might just have something!"

Maximilian dropped his coin on the bank and raced to her.

Chapter 13:
EUREKA!

"What did you find?" Maximilian asked. His heart pounded with excitement.

Madeline slowly removed her paw from the bottom of the coin. Her palm was soiled with dark, wet sand. Throughout the mud sparkled flakes of gold! They shone brilliantly in the sun.

Madeline's eyes shone almost as radiantly as the golden shavings sitting in her hand. Maximilian felt his pulse slow and his excitement fade. Madeline could see Maximilian's expression change to disappointment.

"These waters have been panned by hundreds of prospectors," she said. "This is certainly more than most of them were able to find."

"I guess you're right," Maximilian said. "The thrill of being out here with the possibility of striking it rich can be . . . well, **contagious**." Maximilian returned to his pan downstream.

"I'm having a good time just learning how to stratify with you, Madeline," Maximilian called. The prairie dog had placed the golden flakes carefully in her coat pocket and had resumed panning.

The day wore on. It seemed that the few small gold chips that Madeline had found might be the big score of the morning. A large vulture circled overhead, catching Maximilian's eye.

His pocket watch rang out from the breast pocket of his coat, which sat on the rock behind him. It was now eleven o'clock.

"We need to be mindful of that bird," Maximilian said, glancing skyward. Madeline nodded.

"We should probably think about going back into town," Madeline said. "There will only be more vultures toward noon."

Maximilian agreed. The bird made him nervous. But, he also knew that there were other things that needed to be done. He needed to find the time machine, for example.

"Let's just finish the pans we're working on now and head back into town for some lunch," Madeline said.

A cool breeze blew casually through the long blades of the lowland prairie grass. Maximilian closed his eyes and drew in a deep breath.

Back and forth, round and round, side to side, he continued the rhythmic motions he had been performing all morning. He continued separating the material that he had collected in the bottom of his coin from his final dip.

The soft soil filtered lazily through the screen and made its way back down to the ground. Maximilian was proud of how good he had gotten in just a few hours. He imagined the settlers and prospectors who had traveled hundreds of miles. They had risked everything to stand at riverbanks like these. They did it in the hope that the moistened sod might offer a new beginning.

The face on the front of the coin was coming into view at last. The rest of the mud made its way out of Maximilian's pan.

And then something caught Maximilian's eye. That something was solid and quite out of place.

Maximilian's heart quickened again. The sweat from his forehead trickled down his fur. Squatting by the river, Maximilian grasped a collection of dirt the size of a pencil eraser. He began to wash it clean in the crystal water. The sun began to reveal what Maximilian had only hoped to find.

He worked to clean his discovery. The longer it took, the more he hoped that he had just unearthed the key to saving his home.

Chapter 14:
LUNCH

Maximilian and Madeline quickened their pace as they headed back toward town. They had left the river as soon as Maximilian had shouted for Madeline.

"This absolutely has to stay our little secret," Madeline said, her eyes staring straight ahead. "Are you sure it's safe in your pocket?" she asked for at least the third time.

Maximilian could feel the round golden nugget in his pocket without even reaching his hand inside. It had to weigh several ounces. It had turned out to be somewhat larger than he had originally thought.

"It's as safe as it can be," Maximilian replied. The truth was, his entire body was tense and uneasy about having it on him. But what other option did he have? Despite the heat, Maximilian drew his coat tighter.

"What's next?" Maximilian asked as they entered Silver Springs.

Madeline pointed in the direction of the mercantile in the center of the town.

Floyd's Mercantile? Maximilian remembered seeing the sign tacked carefully over two swinging doors.

"A lot of the buildings here don't have basements or cellars," Madeline said, leading them in the direction of the store. "Reason being that they were constructed so hastily they didn't bother. In many cases, the sod is so hard they felt it would be too time-consuming."

Silver Springs was busy. Horses, wagons, longhorn cattle, and even several stagecoaches added to the bustle of early afternoon.

"A mercantile is bound to have food. I don't know about you, but I'm hungry," Madeline said.

Reaching the foundation of the general store, Madeline appeared to be right. The building had no cellar. Instead, it rested comfortably on large cement blocks almost a foot off the ground.

Madeline and Maximilian walked under the mercantile and into much welcome shade. Maximilian hadn't realized just how long they had been in the sun. His fur was hot to the touch.

They moved toward the middle of the store. The slots between the wooden planked floor surrendered rays of light from above. Both he and Madeline were amazed at how clearly they could make out the individual conversations taking place throughout.

Maximilian carefully removed the golden nugget from his pocket. He and Madeline sat gazing at it.

"I cannot believe that I found this," Maximilian said, looking to Madeline for a hint at what she might suggest they do next.

"From all that I've read," Madeline began, "it is not common to find a piece of gold this size by panning." Several grains of rice and wheat fell directly next to them just as she said the last word.

"More good luck!" Maximilian exclaimed. He cupped his paws to catch the wheat that continued to rain from above. "We're right beneath the grain scale!"

Maximilian and Madeline began scurrying in every direction. They gathered a dozen different seeds, grains, nuts, and kernels. Some of them Maximilian had never even seen before. They found themselves laughing at their good fortune.

They ate until they could eat no more. Then they sat, talking about the moment Maximilian realized he had discovered his piece of gold.

It grew darker beneath the mercantile as Maximilian and Madeline lost track of time. Soon, the sun began to set.

"We should really focus again on finding the stolen wagons," Madeline said.

The sound of thick-soled work boots could be heard directly over them. The steps were so loud that they caught Maximilian's attention.

Overhead, Robert Franklin stood scanning the containers of grain. He held a wooden scooper in his hand.

"Excuse me," Robert said in the direction of a small, elderly fellow who manned a cash register at the store's front. "Do you have sunflower seeds by any chance?" he inquired.

The gentleman acknowledged Robert's question by pointing toward the second aisle of crop seeds.

"I reckon they're in that there aisle," the man said. "We just received a shipment last weekend."

Robert made his way in the direction that the clerk indicated. He paused briefly to read the headline of the *Salt Lake City Chronicle* displayed on a rack at the end of one aisle:

"All Eyes on Promontory Point as East Meets West."

Chapter 15:
THE GOOD NEWS

R obert closed his bag of seeds. He eyed the **rations** that lined the shelves in the mercantile.

"My family and I just got into town yesterday," Robert said, making his way to the clerk. "Started out months ago . . . all the way from Missouri," he said in a proud, confident voice.

"Is that so?" the man asked. He placed Robert's bag on a scale and measured it. "You lookin' for gold or land?" the man asked, in between talking to himself and adding numbers out loud.

Robert was fairly sure the man was just trying to be polite and carry on friendly conversation. He thought the man may be trying to keep him in the store longer to make more purchases. But, it was nice to recount his family's trip.

"Actually, we decided to move out here so I could find a job with one of the railroad companies," Robert said, watching the clerk tally various price tags. He was pretty confident now that the man was simply being polite.

"Is that so?" the elderly man repeated. "Your total for the seeds and the other goods comes to four dollars and thirty-seven cents," he said, finally making eye contact with Robert.

Maximilian and Madeline watched as Robert fumbled with an assortment of coins. Finally, he placed them on the counter in front of the cash register. The man counted them carefully and sorted them into the register drawer.

"Turns out that my timing was perfect," Robert said, unfazed by the older man's lack of interest. "I stopped in the Union Pacific headquarters this morning and signed papers to start with them the beginning of next week."

He could have been talking to himself for all the clerk cared. But knowing that this

job would mean money and opportunities for Martha and Caroline made Robert smile from one ear to the other.

"Is that so?" the store manager said. He turned his back on Robert to stock shelves.

Maximilian looked at Madeline after hearing the good fortune of Robert's job search.

"That doesn't give us too much time then, Madeline," Maximilian said. He started to pace with his hands dug deep in his pockets.

Maximilian's watch chimed seven o'clock.

Robert gathered his bags and made his way toward the street. "Looks like we're headed to Promontory Point," he said as he placed his tattered hat back on his head.

Madeline had her ear pointed in that direction, her eyes widened with the news.

"The caravan is going to Promontory Point!" Madeline said to Maximilian. "They're celebrating the completion of the first **transcontinental** railroad there tomorrow," she said. Maximilian remembered the image of the St. Louis newspaper article.

"We need to see if Garvey and Hal are in Silver Springs. Otherwise, it looks like we'll be moving on to Promontory Point as well," Maximilian replied.

Chapter 16:
GETTING RATIONS

The last kerosene lantern was dimmed and the elderly clerk finished locking the exterior doors before going home for the night.

The commotion from the previous night had returned to the streets of Silver Springs. Maximilian and Madeline waited patiently to collect their own supplies. While they waited, they could hear shouting, laughing, and even the occasional gunshot. Maximilian was more worried than he was letting on to Madeline.

"Let's go!" she said. They squeezed through a knothole in the floorboards and made their way into the store. The dancing light from street lamps outside made for a rather eerie setting inside the store.

"We can't take too much," Madeline said. "We don't have a lot of room in our bags or our pockets."

She was right. If he located the time machine, he had to think about the small space inside the portal. The things he had brought from home and Lincoln's button already took up much of the space. He would make room for his gold nugget but that would have to be all.

A handwritten sign in the front window caught Maximilian's attention.

"Does that sign at the entrance warn customers that they're not allowed to bring firearms into the mercantile?" he asked.

"Yes, it does," Madeline said. "Guns have become a serious problem in places like Silver Springs. Many townships just don't have the sheriffs or deputies to enforce the laws."

Maximilian swallowed hard. He took some comfort in knowing that they would probably be heading farther west come daybreak.

"Come this way," Madeline said softly. Maximilian followed her to a shelf with a sewing needle and navy blue thread. She licked the end of the thread and carefully laced it through the eye of the needle.

"I noticed today that you have a nasty pull in that jacket of yours," she said, taking his coat sleeve in her paw.

Maximilian had forgotten about the damage done to his coat. Madeline had just reminded him of being caught in the railroad tracks in Gettysburg. He could picture Moses now, his strong paws pulling him to safety.

With precise strokes, Madeline made three sweeping stitches in his coat sleeve. The rip slowly disappeared.

"Thanks," Maximilian said. "Where did you learn how to sew?" He looked again at her fine craftsmanship and knew that his mother would approve.

"I learned how to sew and knit from my grandmother," Madeline said. "She taught me a lot of things. She practically raised me," she said. Maximilian realized that this was the most Madeline had opened up about her own story since they had met.

"She's also the one who taught me the importance of reading and learning. She told me to not be scared of taking chances," she said, cutting the thread with her front teeth. "There, you're all set!"

Maximilian and Madeline continued to **scavenge** for supplies and anything else they might need on the next leg of their trip. Suddenly, Madeline froze. She put her fingers to her lips, motioning for Maximilian to stop and listen.

Maximilian heard it. The sound made his blood boil and his heart race at the same time.

"Follow me," Madeline said. Together they climbed the built-in shelves behind the cash register. There, they had a better view to see what they already expected.

They were not alone.

Maximilian stood on the ledge of the shelf, his eyes darting from one end of the store to the other. Soon, he heard the noise again. It was a muffled but familiar sound to the small field mouse.

Maximilian could hear coughing—sickly, suffocating coughing.

Hal was somewhere in the mercantile.

Chapter 17:
NOT ALONE

Maximilian trembled. The fur on his neck stood at attention and his heart threatened to beat out of his chest.

Maximilian and Madeline stood hidden by a glass container. Madeline slowly reached down and squeezed his tiny paw tightly in hers.

Maximilian closed his eyes as he heard the cough muffled in the flannel shirt collar of the wagon thief Hal.

In all honesty, Maximilian was somewhat surprised that the man was still alive. Hal's health had managed to get even worse over the past few days.

Garvey peered out the front window of the mercantile. He turned and whispered nervously in Hal's direction, "Come on, come on. Let's get these supplies and get out of this town."

Hal struggled from one side of the store to the other. He filled a burlap sack with a slew of different items.

"What do you have there, Hal?" Garvey asked, carefully making his way into the shadows of the darkened store. He was careful not to draw attention from passersby.

The light from the full moon shone in slivers through Floyd's Mercantile. The two crooks continued to pack their supplies at a hurried pace.

"Just the essentials," Hal said, beads of sweat visible on his face. "I've got rope, some cans of food, a couple of hunting knives, and some aspirin."

Garvey searched the shelves in the dark, dusty store.

"Don't move," Madeline warned in a low voice. "They'll be gone soon enough after they get everything they need."

Maximilian had managed to bring his nerves under control. He watched the two men closely.

"I've got to go with them," Maximilian said.

"Are you crazy, Maximilian?" Madeline asked in shock.

Garvey paused for a brief moment, his eyes darting around the mercantile.

"Shhh," Maximilian said, placing his pointer finger to his lips. "I have to get back on the Franklin wagon."

Hal grabbed a hammer and a pair of pliers off of a Peg-board near the side counter. He placed them in the bag with the rest of what they were stealing.

Maximilian frantically ran through his options. He had to get to the wagon when the men decided to leave the store. As Garvey went to pick up the bag of supplies, the hammer fell out. A loud bang echoed off the walls. Garvey and Hal froze.

"Leave it!" Hal said. He stumbled toward the back door. "We have to get out of here. They most likely hang thieves in a town like this. Besides, we're going to have to travel all night in order to make it to Promontory Point."

Maximilian could not believe his ears. He scurried down the medicine shelf, past the cupboard, and onto the floor. By the time Garvey and Hal had exited into the dimly lit alley, Maximilian was close behind.

In the alley, the two covered wagons the pair had stolen stood fastened to an empty gunpowder barrel. The four horses drank heavily from a metal trough.

Hal carefully placed the bag in the back of his wagon. Both of the trailers looked identical and Maximilian couldn't tell which he had ridden in the day before.

Finally, Maximilian decided that it was Garvey's ride that carried the time machine. It suddenly dawned on him that he had lost Madeline. Where was she? Was she alright?

With no time to waste, Maximilian raced toward the large iron wheels. He dashed up their rusted spokes toward the wagon's bed.

Although the moonlight was limited in the alley, Maximilian pawed his way through the boxes and crates. Finally, something caught his attention. The time machine was in the corner!

Maximilian breathed a heavy sigh of relief. Then, he realized he wasn't alone in the back of the wagon. He spun around quickly.

"A little help if you wouldn't mind," Madeline said, struggling to heave her bags into the wagon. Maximilian raced over to help her.

He looked at her in shock.

"What?" Madeline asked. "You didn't think I was going to let you continue on this adventure alone, did you?"

The two sat down from exhaustion. They managed to laugh as the two wagons slowly rolled into the street, undetected.

Chapter 18:
MAXIMILIAN'S STORY

The wagon jostled and rocked like it had on the first leg of their trip. Yet, the time machine appeared completely unharmed. Either it was small enough to go unnoticed or Garvey and Hal had not gone through the Franklins' belongings.

Maximilian felt a huge weight immediately removed from his shoulders. Now, he and Madeline rode out of town in silence.

Madeline sat in awe of the time machine. Maximilian caught a glimpse of his journal, the leather binding and red bookmark exactly like he had left them days before.

"What on earth is that, Maximilian?" Madeline asked. She moved toward the time machine to examine it closer.

"It's a long story," Maximilian began, "but I guess we have time." He stood and joined her next to the acorn capsule. Running his paw over the smooth, glazed exterior, he told Madeline everything.

Maximilian shared every stop and every detail of his trip. He even surprised himself with how well he told the story. It had been the first time since Boston that he felt comfortable enough to tell someone else about the time machine.

Madeline said very little. Maximilian could tell that she was trying to believe his tale. Finally, he removed his journal from behind the driver's seat and opened its worn binding.

Maximilian thought for a moment about all the different entries he would have to make about Silver Springs. He would include their stay in the hotel with Martha, stratifying for gold and his lucky find, and the discovery of Garvey and Hal.

Would he even have enough pages to put all of that on paper?

Madeline looked over every inch of the time machine. Finally she said, "I have so many questions, I don't know what to say first. I have seen so many remarkable things on my journey and have read so many staggering things in my books."

Madeline sighed. "But to hear your story and to see the time machine firsthand is the most wonderful experience of my life!"

The two friends talked well into the morning. Neither Maximilian nor Madeline was tired. Maximilian answered each of Madeline's questions. Although one in particular caused him to hesitate. The question lingered in the air as he formed his answer.

"What will you do now?" Madeline had asked. "What will you do now that you've been reunited with your time machine?"

Chapter 19:
THE UTAH SUMMIT

As the morning sun shed light on a new day in Utah, the two stowaways noticed commotion outside. They were so caught up in their own conversation, they had failed to hear the noise. A large number of wagons, horses, and carriages now surrounded them. Soon, their own ride came to a sudden halt.

"We must be there," Madeline said. She pulled the wagon's tarp to peek outside. A crude town of tents and simple shacks dotted the flat landscape. They sat along a long stretch of railroad tie that came to an unexpected stop in the middle of the open land.

It looked nothing like Silver Springs. Maximilian guessed that more people were gathered here.

A group of workers huddled together discussing the day's events. Chinese laborers, Italian **immigrants**, Irish workers, and a German workforce were all represented at the Utah Summit.

"This is amazing!" Madeline said. "I've never seen so many different **ethnicities** in one place at the same time!" Maximilian could do nothing but nod in agreement.

"We're near Promontory Point, just northwest of Ogden, Utah," Madeline said with certainty.

"How do you know?" Maximilian asked. He craned his neck out the back of the wagon for a better view.

"I can picture that framed map back in the hotel hallway," Madeline said. "And we're not too far from Salt Lake City either," she continued.

"Now you're just showing off," Maximilian said. He continued to scan the crowd. "Why do you think we stopped?" he asked. He directed his attention to the front of the wagon where muffled voices could again be heard.

"I have a feeling this is where Garvey and Hal will sell off the Franklins' wagon," Madeline said. She began gathering her belongings.

Maximilian watched as Madeline organized her bags. He thought about what he should do with the time machine. He thought about saying his good-byes now. But he wanted to help bring the two thieves to justice.

"What makes you think that they're going to leave the wagon here?" Maximilian asked. He followed her out of the rear hatch.

Madeline was just a few steps ahead of Maximilian. She talked as she climbed down to the ground. "With the number of reporters here today to see the transcontinental railroad completed, they're bound to be making telegraph transmissions."

Madeline reached the ground and turned to lend Maximilian a paw. He stepped from the wrought-iron wheel spoke. "Robert told the constable in Silver Springs about his wagons being stolen. They wired local authorities who have been searching for Garvey and Hal ever since."

Madeline walked beneath the wagon and looked straight up at the underside. Maximilian tried to figure out what she was planning.

The day's ceremonies unfolded behind them. Two enormous locomotives sat facing each other. The Union Pacific's *No. 119* and the Central Pacific's *Jupiter* stood in the morning haze. They attracted dozens of railroad workers and reporters alike. They all fought for a spot before the driving of the final spike took place.

Maximilian wondered whether or not there was a master of ceremonies to help with organization. Things at this point were looking **chaotic** and uncoordinated.

"I think I have it," Madeline finally said.

"This might just work . . . ," she said, just as Leland Stanford of Central Pacific went to the front of the growing crowd.

Chapter 20:
STANFORD MISSES

Leland Stanford was a **distinguished** man amidst the workers, reporters, and journalists. He was dressed in an impressive suit that had been pressed and tailored. Maximilian could not imagine how hot he must be as the sun continued to rise in the late morning sky.

The crowd was gathering around Stanford. Maximilian and Madeline could not help but move closer. They also wanted to witness the exciting moment that all of the tension was building up to.

Tripods fixed with bulbs and flashes had been mounted near both engines. Photographers began to go under their hoods to prepare for the driving of the final spike.

"Where do you want to go?" Madeline called to Maximilian. Maximilian saw the ideal spot where they could watch history unfold.

"I've got the perfect place," Maximilian said. He ran in the direction of the Central Pacific's *Jupiter.* It sat looming on the track with its brilliantly polished finish. Maximilian and Madeline reached the *Jupiter* and scurried up the wheels and onto the front landing.

Leland Stanford was considered one of the "Big Four" of the Central Pacific Company. David Hewes, a San Francisco construction tycoon, had presented Stanford with a brilliant Golden Spike. It glistened in the bright sunshine. The mere sight of this spike caused a stir amongst the onlookers.

"And I thought my golden nugget was impressive," Maximilian joked.

Stanford raised the Golden Spike and spoke loudly. "It is with honor that I accept this golden spike, engraved with the names of my fellow Central Pacific directors, several special sentiments appropriate to the occasion, and, on the head, the notation 'the Last Spike,'" he announced proudly. Cheers and clapping erupted. Stanford smiled widely, his eyes beaming with pride.

It was truly an extraordinary moment that Maximilian felt blessed to witness. At the same time, **anxiety** continued to build inside him. He knew another trip in the time machine would happen soon.

He fumbled for his pocket watch. It read twelve forty p.m. Maximilian looked over Madeline's shoulder at the Franklin wagon, still sitting by itself where Garvey and Hal had left it. Their team of horses grazed on the tough grass.

A second golden spike was presented on behalf of the *San Francisco News Letter*, while a spike made of silver was the state of Nevada's contribution. Finally, a fourth spike of a combination of iron, silver, and gold was offered to Stanford in honor of Arizona. Maximilian and Madeline watched as all of these ceremonial spikes were dropped into a predrilled tie.

"It strikes me as somewhat peculiar that no spike representing Utah was made," Madeline said. Maximilian had been thinking the exact same thing.

A tall, slender man dressed in work clothes moved through the crowd and handed Stanford a sledgehammer. Maximilian could not help but wonder how Stanford could swing the sledgehammer with the large group assembled around him.

"I cannot believe that we are actually going to witness this, Maximilian," Madeline said excitedly. "I'll surely be reading about this in history books for years to come."

The crowd watched with eagerness as Stanford raised the heavy sledgehammer. It came down forcefully. A collective gasp was shared amongst those in attendance as he missed the spike entirely.

Chapter 21:
WAITING FOR THE FRANKLINS

Maximilian could not believe his eyes! Even more astonishing was that no one in the disorganized mob noticed Mr. Stanford's miss.

Both the spike and the hammer had been wired to transmit the sound of the strikes over telegraph wires to the entire nation. Despite the unsuccessful hit by the Central Pacific executive, the wire operator clicked three dots over the cable . . . "done."

Stanford's face reddened from embarrassment. He reluctantly handed the hammer and the distinguished honor of driving the final peg to the Union Pacific's Thomas Durant. Durant himself gave a half-hearted attempt before relaying the hammer to construction supervisors James H. Strobridge and Samuel R. Reed. Strobridge and Reed took turns driving the last spike.

"Absolutely inspiring!" Madeline said. She placed her paw on Maximilian's shoulder.

It certainly was. Maximilian had witnessed several impressive historical events. He thought that this had to be near the top of his list.

And so, at exactly twelve forty-seven p.m. on May 10, 1869, an ordinary iron spike was driven into a regular railroad tie. This completed an extraordinary transcontinental railroad. Railroad crews of the Union Pacific had pushed west from Omaha, Nebraska. At the same time, teams of Central Pacific crewmen had built their portion of the line east from Sacramento, California.

As Maximilian watched history unfold, he kept a watchful eye on the two **hooligans** who had stolen the Franklin family wagon. Garvey talked with a number of track layers. He spoke with a man wearing a pair of Union-army-issued pants—navy blue with a yellow stripe down each leg. He turned once in a while in the direction of the two stolen wagons. The veteran definitely seemed interested in what Garvey was saying. He consulted his two fellow veterans from time to time.

"It appears our friends are searching for interested customers," Madeline said.

As the day progressed, the temperature began to rise. The plan was to wait until the Franklins arrived from Silver Springs, then reunite them with their stolen supplies. How long they could delay Garvey and Hal from selling their belongings had yet to be seen.

Hal was sweating from fever. He struggled to remain upright. His weight rested heavily on the wagon's rear hatch.

Streams of people were taking turns getting their pictures taken next to the mighty trains. Others were telling stories about the time spent constructing the rail lines through rain, sleet, and snow. In the distance, a line of a dozen or so covered wagons came into view.

"Look!" Maximilian said, pointing.

"Perfect timing," Madeline replied. "It looks as though the Franklins are going to make it to the celebration after all."

Maximilian and Madeline were not the only ones taking notice of the wagon train in the distance. Garvey had started a fast walk back to Hal.

If they decided to leave, would the time machine be going with them?

Maximilian leaped from the *Jupiter*'s running board and began sprinting toward the time machine. Madeline was close behind. She hoped that her plan would work and Garvey and Hal would be stopped once and for all.

Chapter 22:
ONE LAST NIGHT

Maximilian reached the wagon just as Garvey climbed into the driver's seat and grabbed the leather reins. Hal managed to reach the front seat as well. He was barely off the ground when Garvey snapped the reins.

Maximilian, breathing hard, stopped in frustration and kicked at the dirt. Madeline raced to his side and flashed him a devious smile.

"What's so funny? They're going to get away!" Maximilian said, irritated at her laughter.

"Just you wait," she said. She braced herself for what only she knew was coming next.

Garvey steadied himself as the horses **lunged** forward at their driver's command. Their **harnesses** tightened and their muscles coiled.

They drove forward and pulled violently on their hitch.

In one fluid motion, the team of horses ran. And the carriage dropped forcefully onto the ground. A stunned Maximilian jumped. He could not believe his eyes! The horses ran twenty yards before making a sweeping turn and slowing.

Maximilian shook his head and turned his wide-eyed stare to Madeline.

"I don't understand. How did you?" he stuttered. He was unable to find the words to express his amazement.

Madeline turned without saying a word. She displayed a large wooden bolt that had been hidden behind her back.

"It's remarkable just how important each and every nail is to the overall **integrity** of a wagon," she said. She laughed heartily with Maximilian while Robert Franklin and his family arrived with two US marshals.

"Remarkable how a hastily written letter to a nosey store clerk can save the day," Madeline said. Maximilian smiled, realizing that's what had taken her so long to follow him into the alley.

That night, a shooting star ran across the sky. Maximilian and Madeline sat next to a small fire and reflected on the day's events.

Maximilian removed his journal and sharpened the lead on his pencil. Then, he began to write of this leg of his journey.

Soon, Maximilian rubbed his tired eyes. Madeline slept quietly across the fire from him. The cool, clear night made Maximilian draw his coat tighter.

Robert Franklin had joined the Union Pacific crew earlier that afternoon. Plans had been made for Martha and Caroline to continue to San Francisco with the caravan. They would stay with relatives once they arrived.

Madeline had decided to remain with them. She hoped to see the Pacific Ocean and eventually settle down in California.

As for Maximilian, he decided to spend one final evening with Madeline. He would depart at dawn. With any luck, he would be in Tanner's Glen in a few hours.

Maximilian rested his head in his paws, his fingers locked together behind his ears. Another shooting star flew across the heavens, leaving a tail of light in its wake. Maximilian squeezed his eyes shut, held his breath, and made a wish.

Chapter 23:
MOVING ON

Maximilian woke early the next morning. He was ready to prepare the time machine for his next journey. Many of the onlookers from yesterday's ceremony had broken their tents down and were moving west like the Franklins.

Madeline would also be making that trek. She was excited about the idea of a new life in San Francisco. Meanwhile Robert, Martha, and Caroline Franklin were saying good-bye.

Despite the tears that were shed, all three showed remarkable strength. Maximilian felt for them. It made him long for Tanner's Glen and his own mother and sister more than ever.

With renewed strength, Maximilian opened the time machine's portal hatch and secured his belongings.

Now it was Maximilian's turn to say good-bye. Madeline stood at the rear of the wagon, her soft blonde fur blowing in the gentle morning breeze. She watched as Maximilian finished his preparations.

"You know," Madeline said in a quiet, but strong voice, "your friend Abraham Lincoln once said, 'Always bear in mind that your own resolution to succeed is more important than any other one thing.'"

Maximilian smiled and thought it was nice of her to quote a man whom he admired so much. Lincoln's words rang true in so many respects for the pioneers that he had met along this journey out West.

"You have been a great friend to me, Madeline. The wisdom you have shared will stay with me for the rest of my life," Maximilian said. He gave her a big, warm hug.

"Take care of yourself, my brave little mouse," she said and kissed him on the cheek.

Maximilian felt his face warm and tears begin to build. When he undertook this adventure, he never imagined the people he would meet and the life-changing impact they would have on him.

Maximilian climbed into the time machine once again. He closed the door behind him.

The control panel was lit with *15, October, 2013, Tanner's Glen.* He fastened his harness and closed his eyes. In another few seconds it would all seem like a dream.

The time machine began its familiar sequence. Pressure began to build inside the capsule. Maximilian's stomach fluttered with nerves and his ears popped from the force.

When the time machine began to slow down, he gradually opened his eyes. Once again, he undid his restraints and carefully opened the portal with his handkerchief. Suddenly, a strange light came on next to the fuel gauge and a buzzer sounded overhead.

Maximilian's stomach dropped. He fought to make out what the lettering said. He was able to read the words . . . low fuel.

About the Transcontinental Railroad

No figure in American history reflects the spirit of our nation to persevere and to explore more than the pioneer. Covered wagons began making their way across Midwestern plains in the mid-nineteenth century. Many more came after the discovery of gold in California and the surrounding states in 1848.

The trek from east coast to west could take caravans four or more months to complete. Along the way, families determined to make better lives for themselves endured endless hardships and obstacles.

They had no guarantee of a better life waiting for them at their journey's end. But, the promise of their own land and new opportunities were enough to keep the spirit of the pioneer burning bright.

The Transcontinental Railroad was completed at Promontory Point, Utah, on May 10, 1869. That day, the American dream became a reality for more and more people.

A massive building project involved the laying of nearly 2,000 miles of track. The rails were placed over some of the country's harshest land. This coast-to-coast railroad changed the way people and goods traveled throughout the United States. What had taken travelers months before was now reduced to less than a week.

Glossary

accurate - free of errors. Something with errors is inaccurate.

acquaintance - someone you have met briefly.

anxiety - feelings of uneasiness and worry.

canteen - a container for liquid, usually water.

caravan - a group of people traveling together for safety through difficult or dangerous country.

chaotic - of or relating to a state of total confusion.

commotion - loud activity or excitement.

contagious - spreading easily from one person to another.

convoy - a group traveling together.

distinguished - celebrated.

eerie - strange or creepy.

ethnicity - the relation to a group of people based on a common race, nationality, religion, or culture.

frantically - marked by fast, nervous, or worried activity.

frugal - not spending money freely or unnecessarily.

harness - an arrangement of straps used to hold on to or attach something to an animal.

hooligan - a rough person who gets into trouble.

immigrant - a person who enters another country to live.

integrity - the state of being complete and without flaw.

kerosene - a flammable oil.

lunge - a sudden rush forward or reach.

mercantile - a store that trades food and supplies.

notorious - widely known and unliked.

obliged - thankful to someone for doing a kind act or service.

parched - thirsty.

pioneer - one of the first people to settle on new land.

prospector - a person who searches for minerals, especially gold.

ration - a fixed amount of food or goods that are scarce.

scavenge - to search through waste for something that can be used.

sieve - a tool having many small openings that allows liquids to pass through leaving solids behind.

silhouette - the outline of a figure or profile.

transcontinental - crossing a continent.

wallow - to become or remain helpless.

About the Author

Maximilian P. Mouse, Time Traveler was created by Philip M. Horender. Horender resides in upstate New York with his wife, Erin, and their dog, MoJo.

Horender earned his Bachelor of Arts in History with a minor in education from St. Lawrence University. He later obtained his Masters in Science in Education from the University at Albany, the State University of New York.

He currently teaches high school history, coaches swimming, and advises his school's history club. When he is not writing, Horender enjoys biking, kayaking, and hiking with Erin and MoJo.